Kwame's Sound

An Acoustical Engineering Story

Written by the Engineering is Elementary Team
Illustrated by Jeannette Martin

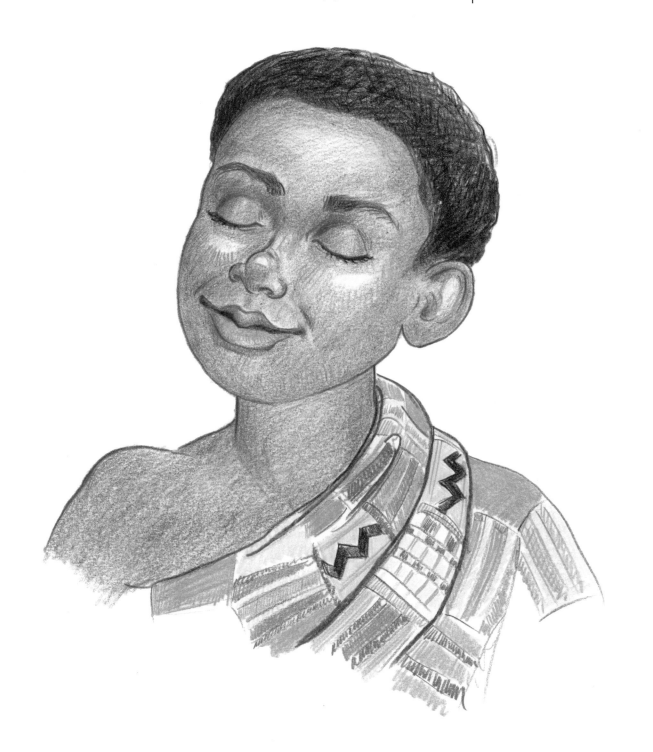

Chapter One | Kwame and His Drum

THWACK boom-boom, mah-dohdoh. Kwame beat on the tightly wrapped skin of his drum. The rhythm thumped through the air like elephants marching through the forest.

With each strike on the drum, he felt vibrations. Louder and faster he played—and the vibrations through his body grew stronger. They felt like the beating of his heart. *THWACK boom-boom, mah-dohdoh. THWACK boom-boom, mah-dohdoh—*

Clap! Clap! Clap!

Kwame's hands paused in midair. He turned towards the bedroom door where he heard his father's applause. Kwame's senses of hearing, touch, and smell were very important to him. He had been born blind.

"That sounds wonderful, Kwame," his father said. His voice was deep and rumbly. "You will perform very well at Odwira this year."

In Ghana, Odwira was a time for people to unite and prepare for the coming year. Last year at the festival Kwame and his cousin Kofi held a large *bommaa* drum steady while their grandfather played a booming rhythm. But this year, Kwame would drum his own rhythm.

"I'm nervous, Father," Kwame admitted. "I wish that Kofi and I could practice together." Kofi lived far away, in the same village as their grandfather. He would be playing Kwame's rhythm with him at Odwira.

"I have a surprise to take your mind off your nerves," Kwame's father said. "We're going to meet a friend of mine."

Kwame thought he knew who his father meant—his coworker, Professor Payne. She was a biologist from the United States who traveled to Ghana for her research. Kwame's father was an acoustical engineer. He used his knowledge of math and science in creative ways to help people solve problems involving sound. He and Professor Payne were working on something called the Elephant Listening Project.

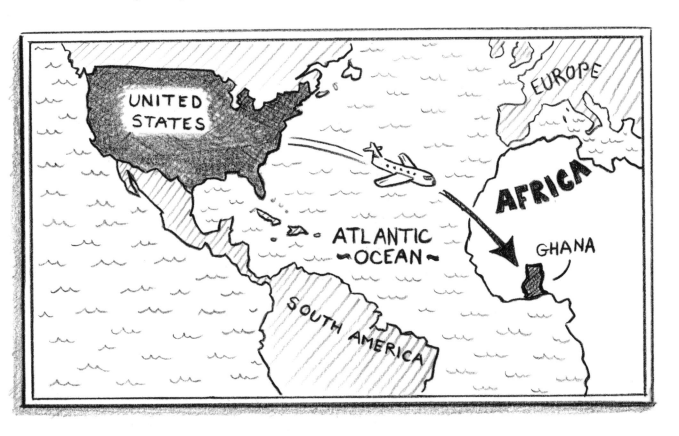

"Is it Professor Payne?" Kwame asked. "Will we get to visit the elephants?"

"Maybe," his father said, "but don't get your hopes up. Even if we go into the forest, we may not be able to hear and record the elephants."

Despite their huge size, forest elephants are hard for scientists to see among all the trees and plants. Scientists like Professor Payne listen to them instead, and use the recordings to track and count the elephants.

For weeks Kwame had been begging his father to take him to meet Professor Payne. He wanted to listen to her CDs of elephant noises. *Maybe I can use these elephant sounds to improve my drumming rhythm*, Kwame thought. He could barely contain his excitement as he followed his father out of the house.

Chapter Two | Listening to Elephants

The city buzzed with activity as Kwame and his father walked through the streets. Stepping into Professor Payne's home was quiet and calm in comparison.

"Hello, Kwame," Professor Payne said in a warm, high voice. "It's nice to meet you." Kwame settled himself in a corner of Professor Payne's office as she popped a CD into the stereo. "Tell me what you think of this," she said. The CD filled the room with loud elephant calls. *Bree-AU-AU-AU-AU-au-aw, breeaw!*

"Are those elephants?" Kwame asked. "They sound like trumpets blasting through the forest."

"They do, don't they?" said Professor Payne. "Here, Kwame, take this statue. Does the elephant's trunk remind you of anything?"

Kwame ran his fingers along the curves of the stone carving. "It's like the bamboo flutes we make in school," he said. Laughing, he added, "Elephants have built-in trumpets, don't they?"

His father chuckled. "That's true. But elephants don't always sound like horns. Elephants make some sounds that humans can't hear."

"How can something be a sound if we can't hear it?" Kwame asked.

"Sounds are really vibrations—something moving back and forth," his father said. "But as a drummer, you already know that."

"Yes!" said Kwame. "Sometimes it feels like the sound of my drum vibrates inside me."

"That happens when the vibrations are slow and low. Some vibrations are so slow and low that you can't hear them," said his father.

"Is it like a whisper?" Kwame asked.

"Well, not really. A sound can be low in different ways. There are sounds that are low in volume, like a whisper. And there are sounds that are low in pitch—that means that the sound vibrations are slow. There can be sounds that are too high-pitched—" he made his voice high and squeaky as he said this—"or too low-pitched," he said in a deep

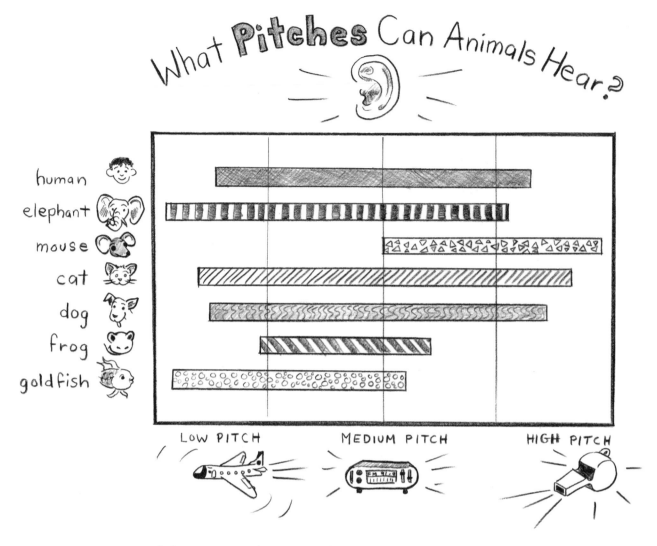

rumbly tone, "for people to hear, but not for other animals. Elephants can hear those low-pitched sounds without any problem."

"I have an idea, Kwame," said Professor Payne. "Would you like to come with us to the field site?"

That is how Kwame got his chance to visit the elephants.

Chapter Three | Into the Forest

Kwame grasped his father's belt and followed him deep into the forest. The birds sang *caw, ka, caw,* above their heads. He heard a frog *ibit, ibit* in the undergrowth.

"We've reached the first listening station," Kwame's father told him. "I'll check the settings on the recording unit."

Kwame walked around the edge of the clearing where they were standing, feeling each tree trunk as he passed. Soon he heard the *thump* of the recording equipment being lowered to the ground behind him.

Professor Payne walked towards Kwame and placed a smooth, metal box in his hand. "Your father helped create these recording units. They help us learn about the different sounds elephants make and how to tell the elephants apart. I can't wait to look at these sound data."

"Look at the sound?" asked Kwame. "How do you look at sound?"

"I'll show you," said Professor Payne. "Do you know what technology is?"

"Technology is any thing that people create to solve a problem," Kwame recited. His father had taught him that.

"Exactly," said Professor Payne. "These recording units are my technology. The recording units take measurements that tell us how loud or soft and how high-pitched or low-pitched a sound is. Scientists like me need a tool to help us understand and analyze the recordings. Those measurements are translated into pictures that we call spectrograms." Professor Payne paused. Kwame heard her rustling the bushes and then heard her scraping something into the dirt.

"I used a stick to draw one example of a sound representation in the dirt. Feel this pattern and tell me what type of sound you think I'm trying to communicate."

Kwame knelt on the ground and Professor Payne helped him move his hand along the dirt ridge. The ridge dipped sharply down, then leveled off in soft, rolling curves.

Kwame sat back on his heels and thought for a moment. "I think this sound starts off very high, like the call of a bird, and then gets lower, like a dog growling. It doesn't remind me of my drum—that would have more sharp ups and downs . . .

"Hey, that gives me an idea!" Kwame exclaimed. "I could make my own kind of spectrogram to communicate my Odwira drum rhythm to my cousin Kofi. If I could create something that represents my music—something that we could both feel instead of see, then we could be sure we were practicing the same rhythm!"

Kwame heard his father's footsteps approaching. "That's a great idea, Kwame," his father said. "Many people write musical notes on paper. Engineering a way to communicate through touching instead of seeing would work well for you and Kofi. You could use the engineering design process to help you."

Kwame's father had told him about the engineering design process before. Kwame knew that he would need to ask questions, imagine solutions, plan and create his design, and improve it. He couldn't wait to get started.

"Kwame," said Professor Payne, "while

we're here in the forest, why don't we walk a little further? Maybe we can inspire your drumming rhythm with some live elephant noises."

Kwame imagined the thump of the elephants' footsteps like the *THWACK* of his drum, and their piercing call like a trumpet. The group walked deeper into the forest. Suddenly, they heard it: a deep, rumbling *Bree-aww*.

"A mother elephant and her calf!" Kwame's father whispered. "I can barely see them through the trees."

Kwame held his breath as he listened. He could hear the soft, high call of the calf. *Bree, bree*. It was the most wonderful sound he'd ever heard.

Chapter Four | Representing Sound

The next day, Kwame sat quietly in his room. He thought about how sound helped him understand the world. He thought about sound as vibrations and about the different sounds he could make with his drum.

His thoughts were interrupted by the sing-song voice of his sister, Afua. "Kwame, come help me make the *fufu* for dinner."

Fufu—a mixture of plantains and yams—was one of Kwame's favorite dishes. He used a large post to mash the vegetables together. As he lifted the post, his sister turned the pot. They fell into a rhythm. *Thump. Slide. Thump. Slide.*

Kwame pictured himself at Odwira, pounding his drum with one hand and sliding his other palm across its surface. *Thump. Slide. Thump. Slide.*

"Afua," Kwame said, "listen." *Thump. Slide. Thump. Slide.* "If you had to represent that rhythm, what would it look like?"

"Kwame, that's silly," she said. "If I draw a picture of those sounds, you won't be able to see it."

"Maybe it doesn't have to be a picture. Maybe it could be a shape that I could feel. Will you try it for me? I'll try one, too," Kwame said.

Afua and Kwame began to work on their designs.

Afua thought that the *thump* would be big and thick—kind of like a yam! The skinny plaintains were long and thin. Maybe they could represent the *slide*.

Kwame was busy scooping some of the *fufu* into a bowl. Remembering what Professor Payne had done, he used a spoon to carve a deep, pointed wave for the *thump* and a shallow swoop for the *slide*.

"Afua, are you ready? Let's test our designs," Kwame said.

Afua led him to her creation. Kwame ran his hands over the yams and plantains. Then he moved to the beginning and felt everything again.

"Is it *thump, slide, slide, thump, thump, slide, slide, thump*?" he asked.

"Yes!" cried Afua. "Now I want to try yours." She giggled as her fingers moved over the sticky *fufu*. Once she reached the end of the pattern, she moved back to the starting point, just as she had seen Kwame do.

"Oh, no!" she cried. "I erased the pattern!"

"Hmm," said Kwame. "That's not good." He giggled. "I bet I couldn't send Kofi *fufu* in the mail, either. I'm going to work on some things in my room."

For the rest of the afternoon Kwame used the engineering design process to help him come up with a representation of his rhythm. He imagined carving a pattern in mud, but he knew hardened mud could be brittle and break. He imagined using wooden beads from one of his sister's old necklaces, but the beads seemed too small to represent the huge beats of his drum. Kwame imagined string and paper, blocks and sticks. Finally, Kwame thought he had a solution. It was time to plan and create his design.

Later that evening, Kwame asked his father to help test his design. Kwame's father sat down with his drum and began to play.

Thump, boom, thump, boom, doh doh-mah.

He paused and turned to Kwame. "What do you think?" he asked.

"It's not quite right. I think I should try to improve my design before I send it to Kofi," Kwame said.

A few days later, after many changes and a few more tests, Kwame was ready to send his homemade spectrogram—a combination of string and blocks—off to Kofi. Now all he could do was wait.

Chapter Five | Testing the Design

Every day Kwame practiced his drumming for Odwira. He was impatient to hear from Kofi. Had he received the package?

Finally one evening, as Kwame was drumming, he heard the high pitched *brrrring, brrrring* of his father's cell phone. "Yao," Kwame's father said. "Where are you calling from?. . . At home? Ah, I see that phone reception has finally reached the village!"

Uncle Yao, thought Kwame—*Kofi's father! He'll know if Kofi got my package.* Kwame waved for the phone, but his father talked on and on with his brother about work and the family.

Finally the conversation shifted. "Kwame has been practicing his drumming as well. . . .I'm sure they will make us very proud at Odwira. . . .well, yes, I think that would be fine.

"Kwame," his father called, "Kofi wants you on the phone."

Kwame carefully took the cell phone that his father handed him. "Hello?" he said. He didn't hear anything. Disappointed, he started to hand the phone back, when a familiar rhythm stopped him. *THWACK boom-boom, mah-dohdoh. THWACK boom-boom, mah-dohdoh.* Kofi was playing Kwame's rhythm!

Kwame beamed with satisfaction. His father and Professor Payne had been right. Using what he knew about sound, along with a little creativity, was all he needed to be an engineer.

Chapter Six | Drumming Together

On the morning of Odwira, Kwame's family prepared to travel to his grandfather's village. He stepped into the *tro-tro*, the city bus, with his arms around his drum and the *kente* cloth of his special Odwira robe cool against his skin.

The *tro-tro* was filled with people and noises, but none of the noises seemed as loud as the sounds coming from within Kwame. His heart beat loudly, his breath rushed in and out, and his knees rattled together. Would he and Kofi really be able to play together, though they'd never practiced in the same room?

His father's hand on his shoulder brought Kwame away from his worries.

"You will do a wonderful job, my son. I know it."

The family stepped off the bus, greeted by the sounds and smells of Odwira. Kwame listened to the hustle and bustle around him. It reminded him of the forest. *Parrots and frogs!* he thought, listening to the calls of women selling their food and crafts. *The elephants*, he thought, hearing the low, drumroll chatter of the crowd, pierced from time to time by a child's cry.

Kofi and Kwame wandered around the village, sampling tangy ground-nut stew and spicy, fragrant meat. The familiar tastes and smells took away Kwame's nervousness and replaced it with joy and excitement.

Soon it was time to drum. Kwame and Kofi sat next to each other and began to play.

THWACK boom-boom, mah-dohdoh, THWACK boom-boom, mah-dohdoh.

Kwame felt the drumming in his hands, in his ears—and in his heart.

Represent a Sound

Have you ever tried to hum a tune, roar like a lion, or growl like a motor? Maybe you've tried to describe a sound with words or write down a song with musical notes. There are sounds all around us and many ways that they can be communicated and described. Your goal is to create a visual representation of a sound, just like Kwame.

Materials
☐ Paper
☐ Pencils, crayons, markers, or colored pencils
☐ A recording device (tape recorder, digital recorder, computer with microphone)
☐ Beads, macaroni, string, and other craft items you might have at home

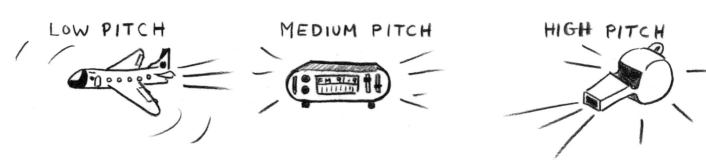

Choose Your Sound
Think of an interesting sound that you have heard and would like to represent. It could be a bird in your garden or an engine on the street where you live. Use a tape recorder, digital recorder, or a computer to record the actual sound you hear. If you can't record the sound, try to memorize it and practice repeating it back to yourself so you can think about all of the properties of your sound.

Design a Representation
Think about the important properties of sound.

☐ Volume: Is the sound loud or soft?
☐ Duration: How long does each part of the sound last?
☐ Pitch: How high or low are the different parts of the sound?

Can you make a drawing in which you represent all three properties at the same time?

Test Your Design

Give your representation to someone to try out. Ask the person if he or she can repeat the sound you illustrated by looking at your representation. You might want to include a key or a guide with your representation so that the person knows which part of your illustration represents each property.

Improve Your Representation

Can you improve your representation system so it is even easier for other people to understand? Try using beads, macaroni, or string so you can feel the representation rather than look at it. Once you have improved your design, try to represent another sound.

See What Others Have Done

See what other kids have done at http://www.mos.org/eie/tryit. What did you try? You can submit your solutions and pictures to our website, and maybe we'll post your submission!

Glossary

Acoustical engineering: The field of engineering concerned with solving problems related to sound.

Afua: Ghanaian name for a female born on Friday. Pronounced *ah-foo-ah*.

Communicate: To convey information.

Engineer: A person who uses his or her creativity and understanding of mathematics and science to design things that solve problems.

Engineering design process: The steps that engineers use to design something to solve a problem.

Fufu: A common food in Ghana, made by boiling and then mashing plaintains (a hard, starchy banana) and yams, or a mix of other starchy vegetables. Pronounced *foo-foo*.

Kente: A woven cloth often worn during ceremonies and special occasions. Pronounced *ken-tay*.

Kofi: Ghanaian name for a male born on Friday. Pronounced *koh-fee*.

Kwame: Ghanaian name for a male born on Saturday. Pronounced *kwa-may*.

Odwira: Festival of purification and unity celebrated by the Akan people of Ghana.

Pitch: A sound property determined by the frequency of vibration.

Represent: To symbolize.

Sound: Vibrations transmitted through matter.

Spectrogram: A series of measurements converted into an electrical signal that is represented by a picture.

Technology: Any thing, process, or system that people create and use to solve a problem.

Tro-tro: A mini-bus used for transportation.

Vibration: A back-and-forth movement.

Yao: Ghanaian name for a male born on Thursday. Pronounced *yah-oh*.